THE NIGHT BEFORE
CHRISTMAS
IN
TEXAS

❧

BETTY LOU PHILLIPS
AND ROBLYN HERNDON

ILLUSTRATED BY
SHERYL DICKERT

GIBBS SMITH
TO ENRICH AND INSPIRE HUMANKIND

C hristmas was coming,
 and Santa was freezing!
A blizzard was blowing!
   The reindeer were wheezing!
The North Pole was covered
   with acres of snow
And the temperature gauges
   read 20 below.

"This cold," Santa cried,
    "is affecting our skills.
We can't be adept when we're
    quaking with chills.
I wish we had hours to
    scour the nation
For a place we could work—
    a second location.

How happy we'd be to have
warm winds surround us.
We wouldn't have icicles
   hanging around us.
Our work would go quickly;
   our spirits would soar;
And our happiness level
   would rise even more!

"My dear Mrs. Claus,
    let's pretend that tonight
We're gazing at tropical
    stars shining bright."
So, warmly ensconced
    in duvets filled with down,
They slept, and they dreamed
    of a faraway town.

In their dreams they were floating,
and flying so high
That they couldn't keep up
  with the sights flashing by.
The bend of a river,
  the crest of a hill,
The cities by night,
  all silent and still.

Then suddenly—dawn!
  The sun rose afar,
Right over the top
  of a lovely lone star!
"I think we're in Texas!"
  Santa shouted with glee.
"Has our dream come to life?
  Could it possibly be?

We're in Austin! A city
so cool and such fun—
This capital claims
to be second to none.
If we want to enjoy
the political fray,
There's the hip *Texas Monthly*
to show us the way.

"Hear that music on Sixth Street!
　　See burnt orange and white
On the exes from Texas—
　　they're the Longhorns, all right!
We're close to the beautiful
　　Hill Country sites,
Where divine days are followed
　　by clear, starry nights."

In a wink, there was Dallas—
   what a fabulous view—
Where architects worked
   as an artist might do
To create a great city,
   with polish and power
In every new edifice,
   every tall tower.

Mrs. Claus was ecstatic!
   "I can't wait to shop!
I'll find Neiman Marcus
   and stay till I drop!
We've a choice of great music
   and football and art,
SMU, the State Fair—and to
   reach them, there's DART!

Fort Worth is the gateway
that leads to the West.
Here cowboys still rope,
and the Stock Show's the best.
The culture is cutting-edge.
Folks make a start
From all over the States
to peruse the fine art.

There's Waco, with Baylor,
  the home of the Bear,
And the Browning Collection,
  and southward from there
You'll see blankets of bluebonnet
  fields in the spring.
The state flower of Texas
  is a beautiful thing!

There's the village of Round Top,
where history speaks.
It's a mecca for finding
uncommon antiques.
San Antonio's River Walk
gives you a view
Of the present, the past,
and the Alamo, too!

Sections of ranchland
are stretching away,
And the riches of Texas
are there on display.
Thousands of cattle are
happily grazing.
The round-up comes later—
that sight is amazing!"

The skyline of Houston
    began to appear.
"Whatever you want,
    chances are that it's here,"
Santa stated. "This city pulls
    out all the stops.
The humidity's high,
    but the people are tops!

"The U. of H., Rice,
   and the medical world
Are there in their glory,
   their banners unfurled.
For the arts, for the sports,
   this place is a winner.
And all the gourmets
   sure can find a great dinner!

The ships in the Channel
   fly flags from all nations,
While Galveston's beaches
   make perfect vacations.
The water is warm,
   and the fishing's a ball.
The cruise ships all know
   it's a great port of call!"

Their dreams took them westward
    to see the Big Bend,
Where views of the fine
    Davis Mountains extend.
They could gaze into space,
    explore Venus and Mars
From that telescope, charting a
    path through the stars.

They dipped toward El Paso,
  which straddles the border.
"What a choice of mouthwatering
  tacos to order!"
They saw the whole Panhandle
  stretched out below
And found Amarillo
  all covered with snow.

The air," Santa said,
 "has a definite nip,
But to see Texas Tech, now,
 is well worth a trip
Down to Lubbock. The campus
 spreads broadly below,
Where the famous Red Raiders
 put on quite a show!

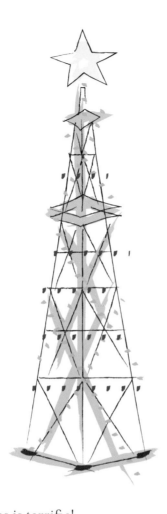

"Texas is terrific!
   That much we can prove.
We know where to go
   if we ever should move.
We've captured the feel
   of this wonderful state.
From space walks to oil wells,
   I think it is great!

I see the moon rising.
It's now time to go
Back up to the Pole, though there's
still too much snow!"
What a dream ride they'd had.
The elves heard them say
They were ready to rise
and get on with the day!

"We've stockings to fill,
    and children to please.
We're up to the task—
    even in a deep freeze!
We found, on our Dream Tour,
    enchantment and charm.
Merry Christmas to Texas!
    You made our hearts warm!"

First Edition
17 16 15 14 13   5 4 3 2 1

Published by
Gibbs Smith
P.O. Box 667
Layton, Utah 84041

1.800.835.4993 orders
www.gibbs-smith.com

Designed and illustrated by Sheryl Dickert
Printed and bound in China
Gibbs Smith books are printed on either
recycled, 100% post-consumer waste, FSC-
certified papers or on paper produced from
sustainable PEFC-certified forest/controlled
wood source. Learn more at www.pefc.org.

Library of Congress Cataloging-in-Publication Data

Phillips, Betty Lou.
  The night before Christmas in Texas / Betty
Lou Phillips and Roblyn Herndon ; illustrated
by Sheryl Dickert. — First edition.
      pages cm
  ISBN 978-1-4236-3509-3
1. Christmas poetry. 2. Texas—Poetry.
I. Herndon, Roblyn. II. Dickert, Sheryl. III. Title.
  PS3616.H453N545 2013
  811'.6—dc23

                          2013007493